HarperCollins®, ◢®, HarperFestival®, and Festival Readers™ are trademarks of
HarperCollins Publishers Inc.
Rainbow Fish: The Good Luck Charm
Text copyright © 2003 by North-South Books Inc.
Illustrations copyright © 2003 by North-South Books Inc.
Printed in the U.S.A. All rights reserved.
Library of Congress catalog card number: 2002104127
www.harperchildrens.com

2 3 4 5 6 7 8 9 10

❖

First Edition

RAINBOW FISH
THE GOOD LUCK CHARM

Text by Sonia Sander

Illustrations by Benrei Huang

 HarperFestival®

A Division of HarperCollinsPublishers

"Attention, class," called Miss Cuttle.
"I hope each of you has a special
dive ready.
Today we will practice for our
diving show."

"Hooray!" cheered Rainbow Fish
and his friends.
They jetted out of the cave classroom.

Tug took his time swimming

over to the Sunken Ship.

He did not like diving.

When Miss Cuttle called,

each fish did a special dive.

Dyna spun.

Puffer flip-flopped.

Rainbow Fish did his famous

loop-the-loop dive.

Tug went last.

He did not have a dive of his own,

so he copied Rainbow Fish.

"That was a very nice dive, Tug.
But you need a dive of your own
for the show," said Miss Cuttle.

"Okay," said Tug.

But he wasn't okay.

Tug was afraid to try a new dive.

13

After school, Rainbow Fish tried
to cheer up his friend.
"I worry about trying new dives,
too, Tug," said Rainbow Fish.

14

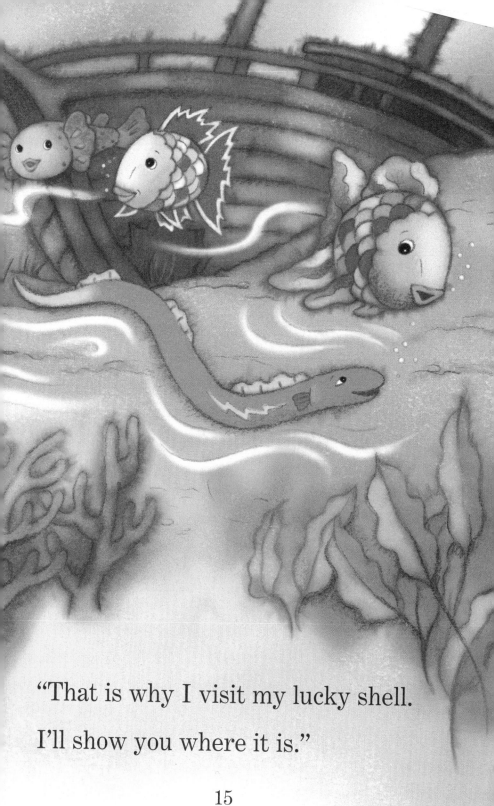

"That is why I visit my lucky shell.
I'll show you where it is."

Rainbow Fish led Tug to the

Oyster Beds.

"All you have to do is swim over to

this shell, touch it, and say:

'I wish I could be a better diver.'"

Tug did just what
Rainbow Fish said.

17

The next day when the class
practiced, Tug was ready.

When it was his turn,

Tug zigged, zagged, and zoomed

into his dive.

Miss Cuttle was impressed.

"It worked!" shouted Tug.

"You were right, Rainbow Fish.

That really *is* a lucky shell!"

Each day before diving practice,

Tug visited the shell.

And each day his special dive

got a little bit better.

The day of the show,

Tug went to visit the lucky shell.

But it was gone!

"Now what do I do?" Tug cried.

Rainbow Fish found Tug hiding.

"Come on," Rainbow Fish said.

"You don't want to miss the

diving show."

But Tug *did* want to miss the
diving show.

"The lucky shell is missing," he said.

"And I can't dive without it!"

"That's not true, Tug," said

Rainbow Fish.

"You're a great diver."

He explained to Tug

that he didn't need the lucky shell.

All Tug needed was confidence.

"But the shell made me a better
diver," Tug said.

"Your dive is better because you
practiced," said Rainbow Fish,
"not because of the shell."
He asked Tug to give it one more try.
"I know you are just as brave
as I am," he said.

Tug was not sure.

But he wanted to be as brave as

Rainbow Fish.

Rainbow Fish and Tug raced to the
Sunken Ship.

The diving show was about to start!

One by one,

each fish did his or her special dive.

Soon, it was Tug's turn.

Tug took a deep breath,

then he zigged, zagged, and zoomed

into his dive.

Everyone cheered.

"You did it!" said Rainbow Fish.

"I knew you could."

But the most important thing

was that Tug knew he could.